For my dad

—Adam

Macie's Mirror written by Adam Ciccio and illustrated by Gertie Jaquet

ISBN 978-1-60537-513-7 (hardcover edition)
ISBN 978-1-60537-537-3 (softcover edition)

This book was printed in October 2019 at Nikara, M. R. Štefánika 858/25, 963 01 Krupina, Slovakia.

First Edition
10 9 8 7 6 5 4 3 2 1

Clavis Publishing supports the First Amendment and celebrates the right to read.

Written by Adam Ciccio
Illustrated by Gertie Jaquet

Macie's Mirror

Clavis
NEW YORK

Meet Macie.

Good enough was never good enough for Macie.

She wanted to be the **best**.

And all the other kids thought Macie was **pretty great** too.

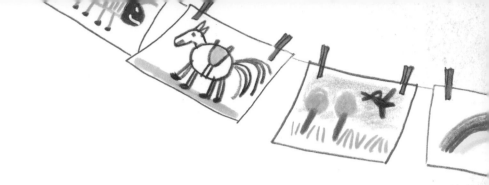

Until, **Penelope** . . .

That night Macie looked in the mirror.
"Maybe I'm not so great."
To her surprise, the mirror answered her!
"Don't worry Macie," the mirror said.
"When you wake up tomorrow
you'll be **perfect**."

Macie woke up the next day
and rushed right to the mirror.
She was expecting to see
a new and **improved** Macie.

But . . .

right in the middle of her forehead was a green spot!

"I can't go to school like this!" Macie cried.

"I'm staying in bed."

As the day went on, more spots started to grow,

a yellow one, a blue one, a red one . . .

Macie asked the mirror, "Why did you do this to me?"
"I am only showing you what you see," the mirror exclaimed.

Macie's dad came up to check on her.
Macie cried, **"Look at me!"**

Together they sat on Macie's bed.
"What I see is someone who is **smart**,
beautiful, and **funny**," said Dad.

"I hope soon you'll see that too.
Because the most important thing is
that you love you."

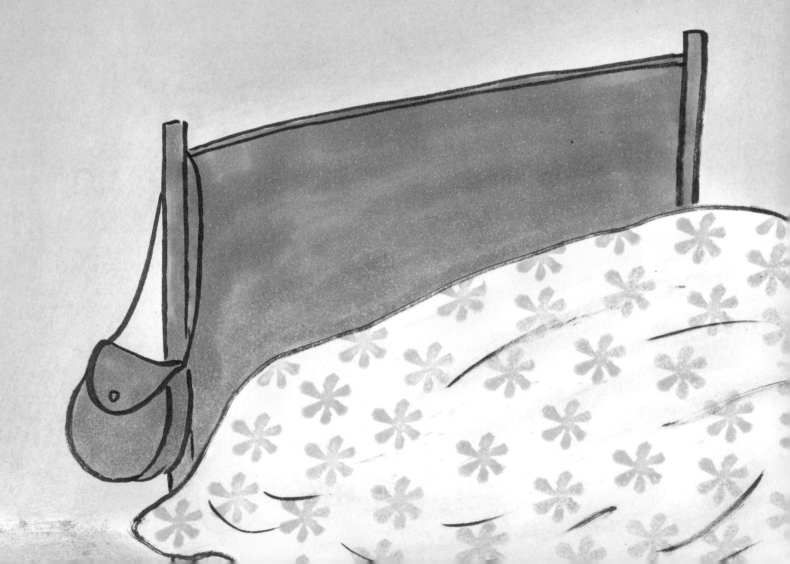

Macie took a look in the mirror again,
her father's words swimming in her head.
The most important thing is **that you love you . . .**

And slowly her image started to change.
When she looked in the mirror, all the spots were gone.
She wasn't perfect. But she loved what she saw.

Macie went back to school the very next day.
She knew she wasn't perfect,
but that was okay!

And as for her mirror, well . . .
She threw it away.